Dead Cool

by

Peter Clover

Illustrated by Peter Clover

D0994707

Clover, Peter

Dead cool / by
Peter Clover /
illustrated by
                  JF

1556424

You do not need to read this page –
just get on with the book!

First published in 2005 in Great Britain by
Barrington Stoke Ltd, Sandeman House, Trunk's Close,
55 High Street, Edinburgh EH1 1SR

This edition based on *Dead Cool*, published by
Barrington Stoke in 2003

Copyright © 2005 Peter Clover
Illustrations © Peter Clover

The moral right of the author has been asserted in
accordance with the Copyright, Designs and
Patents Act 1988

ISBN 1-842993-27-5

Printed in Great Britain by Bell & Bain Ltd

Meet the Author and Illustrator
Peter Clover

What is your favourite animal?
I love cats
What is your favourite boy's name?
Bonehead
What is your favourite girl's name?
Jordan
What is your favourite food?
Roast potatoes and Yorkshire pudding
What is your favourite music?
American Soul and R&B
What is your favourite hobby?
Talking

For Stephen and Yvette

Contents

Chapter 1
Pretty Polly

Sammy wanted a dog. He wanted a dog very badly.

He didn't want just any old dog. It had to be a huge Great Dane. But Mum said he couldn't even have a little dog. You see, they lived in a very small flat at the top of an old house right on the edge of the sea. Below them was Mr Hackbone's shop, where he sold all sorts of things that were old and interesting.

"We can't keep a dog up here in the flat!" said Mum. "We don't have a garden. Dogs need gardens. Dogs dig. It wouldn't be right. Anyway, Mr Hackbone wouldn't like it!"

"A cat, then!" begged Sammy. "How about a huge big tomcat? Cats don't need gardens. Lots of people keep cats in flats. Cats love small spaces – ask anyone!"

"Not a cat," said Dad. "Never! Cats have sharp claws. A cat up here would rip up this place in ten seconds. How about a nice goldfish?"

"Boring," said Sammy. "And I'd get dizzy watching it swim round and round all day. So dizzy that I'd faint." He fell to the floor with his eyes rolling.

"A nice budgie, then?" said Mum.

"Budgies aren't cool," Sammy told her. "How about an ostrich? Or an eagle?"

In the end they chose a parrot, a bright green talking parrot. Dad went out and got it the next day.

Mr Hackbone didn't mind them having a parrot in the flat. He even gave Mum an old brass birdcage which he'd found years ago in the cellar under the shop.

The cage was great. But the parrot was no use at all. You see, it didn't talk. Not a peep! Not a squawk! Zilch! Nothing!

"I thought we were told this parrot could talk!" said Sammy crossly.

"Give Polly time," said Mum. "Let her get used to us and the flat. I expect she'll have lots to say in a day or two." Mum pushed

out her lips and blew kisses to Polly through the bars of the cage.

Polly fluffed up her feathers. Then she leaned back so far she fell off her perch. She swung upside down with her head in the seed tray.

"This bird's daft," said Sammy. "She's bonkers. Can't even stay on her perch properly. Some parrot!"

Polly dropped to the floor of her cage, got up, gave a loud squawk and began to scratch around in the grit and sawdust.

Sammy popped a grape through the bars and watched Polly kick it around like a football. Then she picked it up and peeled it with her beak. Polly liked grapes.

"Clever Polly," said Sammy. The parrot looked at him with beady black eyes. Then she did a poo!

"Pretty Polly. Pretty Polly," squawked Sammy. The parrot put her head to one side and waited for another grape.

After nine grapes, Sammy gave up. Apart from the odd squawk when she saw herself in the mirror, Polly said nothing.

"Give her time," smiled Mum. "I expect she's shy."

But three days passed and Polly hadn't said a word.

The next day, which was a Thursday, Sammy came clomping up the stairs to the flat and crashed into the small living room. He threw his school bag onto the settee.

"Pretty Birdie," said a voice from behind him. It was a squawky parrot voice, and it came from the corner of the room where Polly's cage stood.

Sammy spun round. Could it be true? Had Polly spoken at last?

Sammy dashed across the room and looked into the cage. He gasped. For there, sitting on the perch, was not just one bright green parrot, but two!

Chapter 2
A Feathered Phantom

"Wow!" said Sammy. At first he thought that Mum and Dad had got him another parrot. But when he looked closer, Sammy got quite a shock.

For there was something very odd about this second parrot. It *seemed* to be there all right, but it looked more like a fuzzy picture of a parrot than a real one. And when Sammy stared at it closely, he could see right through it.

Polly was thrilled. She was gripping her perch so hard that her eyes almost popped out. The second parrot snuggled up to her and cooed as he said her name over and over again.

"Polly, Polly. Pretty Polly. Pretty Polly."

Sammy's parrot was shy. This new one was bold and brassy – a bit of a show-off, in fact.

"Pretty Polly. Who's a pretty Polly, then? Phwoaarrhhh!" The new parrot squawked again and again. Really loudly.

Sammy opened his mouth but no sound came out. He wanted to say something ... anything. But, before he could think what to say, the second parrot vanished into thin air. A silver mist floated and twisted upwards through the bars of the cage. Then, poof! The other parrot was gone.

Sammy didn't tell anyone. But that night he couldn't sleep. He kept getting up, creeping into the living room and checking on Polly.

"I must check this out!" said Sammy to himself.

Was it all a dream? Had he really seen a second parrot, a ghost one? At last, worn out, Sammy fell into a deep sleep. Morning came. Mum yelled from the kitchen, "BREAKFAST!"

Sammy jumped out of bed and ran into the living room. Polly was in her cage. And so was the other parrot. The ghost one. He was sitting really close to Polly and pushing her against the side of the cage so that her feathers stuck out through the bars.

Sammy rubbed his eyes. Was he dreaming? No – the other parrot was still there. This was cool. Dead cool! "Where did you come from?" asked Sammy softly, so that Mum wouldn't hear.

"Captain Crabmeat's a clever boy," squawked the parrot, looking at Polly. "Polly, Polly. Pretty Polly. Cor, give us a kiss, me darling!" This parrot could really talk. It was brilliant!

Then Mum called again from the kitchen. And as Sammy spun round he saw a monster cat. A huge red tom. It was lying in the armchair.

"A CAT!" Could this be true? Sammy shivered. He suddenly had seen its fuzzy red fur. Like the second parrot, the cat was like a hazy ghost. But it *was* there! Sammy could see it as plain as day.

"Sammy!" Mum called again. "Breakfast!
Now!"

Sammy took one more look at the cat and dragged himself off to the kitchen.

He had just sat down at the table when the cat came into the kitchen after him. It jumped onto his lap, where it settled. Sammy felt its warm body against his legs. The cat dug in its claws. Sammy stroked its soft red fur.

Mum and Dad said nothing. It was clear that they couldn't see the cat. Just like the parrot, it could only be seen by Sammy.

"Shiver me timbers. Polly, Polly. Pretty, pretty, Polly," Captain Crabmeat was squawking loudly in the next room. But Mum and Dad couldn't hear a thing!

Sammy ate his breakfast fast and got ready for school. He left the red cat asleep on his bed. It was really hard to leave the house that morning. Sammy wanted so badly to stay at home and find out just what was going on. He wanted to see if the cat would vanish again, like the parrot. And he wanted to see if anything else would arrive out of thin air.

Chapter 3
An Unexpected Visitor

The school day dragged on. It was Friday and they were going home early for half term. They could all leave at 3 p.m.

Sammy ran all the way home. He ran up the stairs to the flat and let himself in with his key.

Mum worked part-time in Mr Hackbone's shop. She wouldn't come up to the flat before 3.30 p.m. So Sammy had half an hour all to himself.

First things first. Sammy dashed into the living room. Polly and Crabmeat were kissing and cuddling in the corner of the parrot cage. Polly seemed to be enjoying herself.

"Polly, Polly. Pretty Polly," squawked Crabmeat as Sammy came into the room. "Land ahoy. Strike up the Jolly Roger. Pieces of eight. Pieces of eight."

Once Crabmeat started to talk he just wouldn't shut up. He seemed to be very excited about something.

All at once, Sammy felt an odd fizzing in the air.

He looked around for the red cat. But the big tom wasn't in the living room. In fact, he couldn't see it anywhere. Sammy had left his bedroom door open a crack in case the big cat wanted to go for a walk. But that seemed a stupid idea now. After all, if the cat could appear out of thin air, then it could pass through walls and doors anytime it wanted. Sammy checked his room. The cat wasn't there!

Maybe it's in the kitchen? thought Sammy. But no. He looked everywhere in the flat, which didn't take long, then gave up and went back to his room again. This time, as he pushed open the door and stepped inside, Sammy gasped.

There, lying on his bed, was not just *one* cat, but two huge great toms, one red and one striped. And there was more ... much more. Sitting in a chair was a young lad. He was flicking through Sammy's footie mags.

Sammy was amazed. The boy dropped the mags and stared back at Sammy from across the room.

This boy was about the same age as Sammy, but pale grey all over. And Sammy could see right through him. He wore shabby trousers, cut off shorts, and a tatty shirt. His hair was long, matted and tied back in a rat's tail. His bare feet were black and grubby. And there was a smell of salt and seaweed coming from *his* corner of the room.

The boy spoke first.

"Ahoy, shipmate!" He sounded bright and cheerful. He was not at all shocked or amazed, as Sammy was. "My name's Smitty. Welcome aboard," he added, with a cheeky grin.

Sammy was stunned. "Hi," was all he could say.

"Strike up the Jolly Roger," squawked Crabmeat from the living room. "Pieces of eight. Pieces of eight."

The boy laughed and so did Sammy. The crazy parrot seemed to have broken the spell.

"Where the flipping heck did you come from?" Sammy said at last. "And what are you doing here ... in my room?" Sammy didn't mean to sound so rude. But it just sort of came out that way. He hoped that he hadn't upset the boy. After all, it was quite a shock for him to find a ghost sitting in his room.

But Smitty was upset. The bright cheerful grin faded. It was as if his light had gone out.

"Sorry!" said the boy. "I didn't think you'd mind if I dropped in." Then he closed his eyes and faded into thin air. All that was left was a faint smell of the sea.

"Come back!" yelled Sammy. "It's all right. Come back! You can stay. I *want* you to stay." But the boy didn't come back. He had gone.

Sammy spun around to face the bed. The two cats had gone too! He ran into the living room. Polly sat alone on her perch. She looked confused and upset.

"Pretty Polly. Pretty Polly." It was the first time that Polly had ever spoken. But it was a sound filled with sadness. Crabmeat had gone too!

Chapter 4
Shiver me Timbers

Mum came up from the shop at exactly 3.30 p.m. and sent Sammy out to buy bread and milk at Supa Shopper. Sammy set off slowly. All the time he was thinking about Smitty and the other strange events of the past few days.

Sammy wished that he'd been kinder to the ghost in his room. Would the boy ever come back? He might. After all, Crabmeat had already come back twice!

Sammy still didn't tell his parents about the ghosts' visits. They would think he had made up the whole story because *they* couldn't see anything. And everyone knows that ghosts aren't real!

On the way back from Supa Shopper, Sammy stopped in the street and looked up at the windows of their flat. Then he studied the whole of the front of the house. It was if he was seeing it for the first time. It was very, very old.

Just how old was the house? It must be very old indeed. The crooked windows of Mr Hackbone's shop had tiny glass panes. And there were four numbers carved above the door. It looked like a date: 1758. Wow! This house really was old!

Sammy had never noticed the date before. He wanted to know more and decided to ask Mr Hackbone about it in the morning. But before he could do so, something much more odd happened!

Sammy was sitting in bed that night reading his footie mags, when his nose started to twitch. There was a smell of fish and seaweed in his room.

He took a long, deep sniff. And when he looked up, he gasped. There, at the end of his bed, was the ghost boy, Smitty.

Sammy was shocked, but pleased. The two big cats had come back too and were padding around on his bed. They plonked themselves down on his soft pillows.

Then he heard Crabmeat squawking next door.

"Hello!" Sammy said softly to Smitty. This time he was careful to sound nice and friendly. "I'm sorry about last time you were here. I'm glad you've come back!"

Sammy wanted to talk and find out why Smitty came to see him. It was all so odd.

"I hope you don't mind," grinned Smitty. His eyes shone. "But I've got a few more friends with me."

What did he mean? But before Sammy had time to ask, 11 sailors from the good ship the *Black Crow* stepped through his bedroom walls.

There was a strong smell of herring and the sea. Somewhere Sammy could hear creaking sounds like those of an old ship. He stared hard at the pirate crew. For that's what they were ... *PIRATES*.

There was Bacon, the ship's cook, Doc Bones, Squire Delaney and Boris the Bosun. There were seven sulky deck hands, all dressed in funny clothes with cut off trews and flashy jerkins. Sammy gasped. He was very excited.

Chapter 5
Red Beard the Really Rotten

Sammy sat up in bed and gazed silently at the amazing sight before him.

"Is it all right if we stay?" asked Smitty. "We won't get in the way. We won't take up any space and no-one can see us except you and your parrot!"

But what if Mum finds out? thought Sammy. *She'd go ballistic. She'd hit the roof. She'd want to get rid of them all at once.*

But it was almost time for bed, so Sammy didn't think it would matter if they stayed for just one night. He didn't say that! He just nodded his head at them. Suddenly, the pirate crew started to sing loudly. "Yo ho ho and a bottle of rum," they sang. Sammy put his fingers into his ears. Mum and Dad must be able to hear that! They were only in the next room watching TV. In a moment they would come rushing into his bedroom. But they didn't.

Mum and Dad just can't see or hear ghosts, Sammy thought.

At last, the crew stopped singing, and squashed themselves into Sammy's bed. The amazing thing was that they didn't take up much space at all. Then the talking began. Sammy told them all about school. But there were so many questions he wanted to ask them. Who were they all? Where did they come from? What did they want?

This is what they told Sammy:

250 years ago, in a time of sailing ships and pirates, Smitty and his friends were cabin boy and crew aboard the *Black Crow*. She was a pirate ship that roamed the Seven Seas.

Crabmeat was the *Black Crow*'s lucky mascot. And the two big cats were the ship's rat catchers. For years the *Black Crow* sailed the Seven Seas, robbing the trade ships. But the crew didn't want to be outlaws. They wanted to be jolly sailors. They had been made to be pirates by the evil Red Beard the Really Rotten.

The crew were scared stiff of Red Beard the Really Rotten. They told Sammy how one day they had planned a mutiny. They got Red Beard the Really Rotten very drunk on rum. Then they made him walk the plank.

But almost at once there was a disaster. The ship hit a big rock and the *Black Crow* sank. Everyone on board was drowned. But that wasn't the end of it. There was much worse to come. The crew all turned into ghosts. Ever since they had been roaming the world, unable to rest for fear that Red Beard would catch them. He had been chasing them for 250 years. He wanted his revenge.

Wow! Could this be true? "But why have you come here?" Sammy asked. Sammy was starting to get worried. "Won't Red Beard

the Really Rotten follow you and come here too?"

The crew looked shifty.

Smitty spoke, "It was Crabmeat who found the way to you through the mist. It seemed a safe place. Once he had got safely through onto your side we sent the cats. Then I came."

"But we're still not sure how safe it is," added Squire Delaney. "We've never found a hiding place like this before! And we're so tired. We can't keep running for ever. We just need a rest."

Has the brass birdcage got something to do with this? Sammy thought. *After all, the cage is very old. And Mr Hackbone told Mum that it had been in his cellar for years. In fact, it might have been there since 1758.*

No-one seemed to know where the cage had come from. But did it matter? The pirate crew were what mattered now! They were right there tucked up in Sammy's bed. And what was going to happen next?

Chapter 6
A Storm is Brewing

The pirates told wild stories for hours but at last Sammy fell fast asleep. He was quite pleased to find his bedroom empty when he woke up the next morning. He felt worn out.

Sammy could smell grilled bacon. He rubbed his eyes. Perhaps last night had just been a fantastic dream after all! He would pop down to see Mr Hackbone after breakfast, and ask about the old house *and* the parrot cage. Was there a link?

He pulled on his trousers and a T-shirt. Then he padded barefoot into the kitchen.

The first thing that Sammy saw was Smitty, sitting in *his* place at the table, with Crabmeat on his shoulder.

Then he felt something soft and furry against his feet. Looking down, Sammy saw the two huge cats rubbing themselves against his legs.

"Morning, Sam," said Mum. "Breakfast is ready." She flipped two eggs and some crispy bacon onto a plate. Smitty licked his lips. He hadn't eaten for years. Not for 250 years. And he'd *never* seen bacon like this!

Sammy gave Smitty a nod and a signal to move into the next chair. Then Sammy sat down.

Dad came in with his newspaper and plonked himself down on the other side of the table. Then, all at once, the crew of the *Black Crow* stepped through the wall behind Dad. There they stood, bending over the table, drooling at Sammy's plate of bacon and eggs.

"Shiver me timbers. Ship ahoy! Pieces of eight! Pieces of eight!" Crabmeat landed on Sammy and squawked loudly in his ear. Dad didn't even notice. He just went on reading his newspaper. Mum poured the tea.

"It's a bit warm in here this morning," she said. "No air." And Mum flung open the window. She looked up at the sky. "Those

clouds over the sea are so black," she said. "There must be a big storm coming. Goodness, it's stuffy in here."

And I know why, thought Sammy. He didn't say anything. He just sat there and his face went pale. The air in the flat did feel a bit thick. In fact it felt so thick, you could almost cut it with a knife. Or a cutlass.

Sammy didn't eat any of his breakfast. He sensed that Smitty and the pirate crew had something to do with this stuffy feeling and the looming storm. He stared past his dad at Smitty, who was standing behind him. He was still looking hungrily at the great plateful of bacon and eggs.

"This bacon smells a bit funny," said Dad. "A bit like … seaweed!" He lifted a whole rasher on his fork and took a deep sniff. The smell of the sea filled the small kitchen. Then the bacon vanished. And

Smitty stood, licking his lips. Crabmeat squawked and Dad just stared at his empty fork.

Outside, the sky grew even darker. All at once the crew became restless. They looked at each other. They were worried. The storm was right above the house.

Sammy's hair stood on end. Then a deep rumble behind the black clouds shook the windows and a flash of lightning lit up the room.

Mum gave a scream. Crabmeat fell off Sammy's shoulder. And there was Red Beard the Really Rotten, standing at the open kitchen door, wild with rage.

He wore a thick grey coat and a three-cornered pirate hat. He had one wooden leg and a metal hook in place of a hand. He also wore a patch over one eye. It seemed to Sammy that there was quite a lot of him missing. But what was left was very scary.

250 years of anger and fury oozed out of every part of his body. Smoke came out of his nose and red flames crackled from his big, bushy beard. The ghost of Red Beard the Really Rotten was six foot tall and as wide as a barn door. They looked at him

with terror. The air popped and fizzed around him.

Then Red Beard began to grin, an angry grin that flashed like lightning all over his ugly face.

The crew gasped. And Smitty's eyes grew as big as plates.

Red Beard glared at his long-lost crew. "At last!" he yelled. He smelt of stale kippers. "At last! Revenge is mine!"

Chapter 7
The Final Revenge

Mum slammed the kitchen window shut.

"What's that horrible smell?" she said, looking at Dad. Red Beard gave another roar and pulled a pistol from his belt.

Sammy hid under the table.

"Sammy, what are you doing?" said Mum. "It's only an electric storm!"

Thunder exploded over the house as Red Beard fired his pistol. The first shot went right past Dad's ear and broke the teapot. Mum yelled as Smitty and the pirate crew crashed past her and tried to hide inside the fridge.

The lightning flashed again and Dad jumped to his feet. He had never seen a storm that smashed china before. Red Beard fired another pistol shot and a teacup exploded. Sammy peered out from under the table. It was all too much.

Then something even more amazing happened ... A woman came out of nowhere and was there in the room. She was short and dumpy. She wore a cotton cap and a long apron down to the floor. Her face was red and plump and she waved a soup ladle in her hand, like a club.

"Robert Red Beard," she yelled, in a voice that could sink ships, "where have you been? You ran off and left me with a whole lot of kids to feed and a house that was falling down. How do you explain that, husband?"

The fridge door opened a crack and Smitty stuck his head out, just in time to see Mrs Red Beard take a swipe at her husband with the huge soup ladle. Red Beard the Really Rotten ran for his life as the little woman chased him out of the kitchen. "You ran off to sea and left me to a lifetime of hard work and misery," she yelled after him. "You'll not get away from me, you fish-faced sea dog. I'll really get you this time."

Red Beard the Really Rotten didn't stay around any longer. He forgot all about revenge. In a flash he had stumped down the hall at 100 miles an hour, and was gone for ever, with Mrs Red Beard chasing after him. He left nothing behind but the smell of rotten fish.

Outside, the storm was over and the sun had come out. Sammy knew that Smitty and the crew would never be bothered by Red Beard again. One by one they came out of the fridge and slipped out of the room.

Mum and Dad were busy sweeping up the mess on the table and floor with a dustpan and brush.

"Phew! I've never known a storm like it," they were saying. Sammy slipped away to his bedroom.

Smitty was in there with the pirate crew. They were laughing.

"Fancy old Red Beard being chased off like that by his own wife."

"She did look mean, didn't she?" grinned the Squire. "He'll spend the rest of his miserable days keeping out of *her* way, that's for sure."

The sun shone in through the bedroom window as one by one the crew said goodbye and faded back into the grey mist from where they had come.

"Come on, lads. We've got to find a ship," said Boris the Bosun. Some went through the walls. Some floated up through the roof. And some faded into the floor.

Crabmeat was the last to go. With one last squawk and one last nuzzle with Polly, he pecked her on the head and vanished.

Sammy felt really sad. It had been so exciting having Smitty and his pirate pals around. And now they had all gone.

Polly looked sad too. She puffed out her feathers and shut her eyes tight. She was missing Crabmeat as much as Sammy was missing Smitty. *I must do something*, Sammy thought. *I know. I'll clean and polish Polly's cage.*

As Sammy began to rub and polish, he suddenly saw a small nameplate on the base of the cage. At first there didn't seem to be anything written on it. But, when Sammy rubbed a bit harder, the name *Captain Crabmeat* shone through, bright and clear.

Sammy smiled to himself. Now it all made sense. He didn't have to ask Mr Hackbone after all. It was Crabmeat's cage which had got them all through from the other side. And it was Polly who had given the cage a new life.

Sammy carried the cage through into his bedroom. From now on, Polly would live there.

"Ahoy there, shipmate!"

Sammy nearly dropped the cage. He spun round. It was Smitty and the pirate crew. Or at least their heads, which were poking through Sammy's bedroom wall.

"We think we'll stay after all," they grinned. "We thought it might be more fun to hang out here for a while. That is, if there's room on the ship?"

Sammy laughed. "How much room does a ghost pirate crew take up?" he asked.

"Room enough to play a few tricks," grinned Smitty. "Now tell us all about this place called school again."

Sammy hugged himself. He wasn't going to tell anyone about this. He was going to keep Smitty and the pirate crew a secret. And he was going to take them to school. That was for sure. What a really cool idea. Dead Cool! And Sammy couldn't wait!

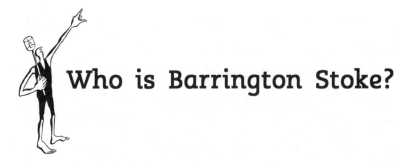

Who is Barrington Stoke?

Barrington Stoke went from place to place with his lamp in his hand. Everywhere he went, he told stories to children. Some were happy, some were sad, some were funny and some were scary.

The children always wanted more. When it got dark, they had to go home to bed. They went to look for Barrington Stoke the next day, but he had gone.

The children never forgot the stories. They told them to each other and to their children and their grandchildren. You see, good stories are magic and they can live for ever.

If you loved this story, why don't you read ...

The Best in the World

by Chris Powling

Have you ever wanted to push yourself to the limit? Lucas and Jeb are ready to do the "Triple" and become the best trapeze artists in the world. But will they risk their lives to follow a dream?

4u2read.ok!

You can order this book directly from our website
www.barringtonstoke.co.uk